AND THE
MORPHING
MOVIE STAR

WRITTEN BY
MICHAEL ANTHONY STEELE

ILLUSTRATED BY
GREGG SCHIGIEL

BATMAN CREATED BY
BOB KANE WITH BILL FINGER

STONE ARCH BOOKS
a capstone imprint

Published by Stone Arch Books, an imprint of Capstone.
1710 Roe Crest Drive
North Mankato, Minnesota 56003
www.capstonepub.com

Library of Congress Cataloging-in-Publication Data
Names: Steele, Michael Anthony, author. | Schigiel, Gregg, illustrator.
Title: Batman and the morphing movie star / by Michael Anthony Steele ; illustrated
    by Gregg Schigiel.
Description: North Mankato, Minnesota : Stone Arch Books, a Capstone imprint,
    [2021] | Series: Dc super hero adventures | "Batman created by Bob Kane with Bill
    Finger." | Audience: Ages 8-11. | Audience: Grades 4-6. | Summary: Super-villain
    Clayface tries to stage a comeback as a movie star, but when Batman and his
    sidekick, Batwing, link him to a series of bank robberies, it is time for action.
Identifiers: LCCN 2020026193 (print) | LCCN 2020026194 (ebook) | ISBN
    9781515882145 (library binding) | ISBN 9781515883234 (paperback) | ISBN
    9781515891789 (pdf)
Subjects: CYAC: Superheroes—Fiction. | Supervillains--Fiction. | Actors and
    actresses—Fiction. | Motion pictures—Production and direction—Fiction.
Classification: LCC PZ7.S8147 Bao 2021 (print) | LCC PZ7.S8147 (ebook) | DDC
    [Fic]—dc23
LC record available at https://lccn.loc.gov/2020026193
LC ebook record available at https://lccn.loc.gov/2020026194

Designer: Hilary Wacholz

TABLE OF CONTENTS

CHAPTER 1
AND . . . ACTION! 6

CHAPTER 2
BEHIND-THE-SCENES BANK ROBBERY . . 17

CHAPTER 3
PERFORMER PLOT TWIST 31

CHAPTER 4
REAL-TIME REMAKE 44

CHAPTER 5
STUNT DOUBLE TROUBLE 55

While still a boy, Bruce Wayne witnessed the death of his parents at the hands of a petty criminal. The tragic event changed the young billionaire's life forever. Bruce vowed to rid Gotham City of evil and keep its people safe from crime. After years of training his body and mind, he donned a new uniform and a new identity.

He became . . .

BATMAN™

CHAPTER 1

And . . . Action!

The main door of the office building burst open. A blond man, dressed in a tuxedo, dashed out and sprinted across the sidewalk. He slid over the hood of a sleek sports car and landed on the other side. He reached for the car door.

Five men in ski masks ran out of the building after him. One jumped into the air, somersaulted over the car, and landed beside the blond man.

WHAM!

The masked man kicked the car door shut, keeping the blond man from escaping. Without missing a beat, the blond man dropped to the ground and swept the legs out from under the attacker.

As the other four surrounded him, the blond man in the tuxedo blocked punches and dodged kicks. Meanwhile, the first attacker got to his feet and grabbed the blond man from behind. The blond man flipped the attacker over his shoulder. He smashed into two of the masked men, knocking them to the ground.

The blond man took out the last two attackers with one kick. Then he adjusted his bow tie as he stepped over the unconscious men. He opened the car door and slid behind the wheel.

"And . . . cut!" shouted the director.

The masked attackers got to their feet as the blond man exited the car. Spectators, gathered on the sidewalk, applauded the exciting action scene. Bruce Wayne was among them. The billionaire was still clapping as one of the masked men strolled up to him. He pulled off his ski mask to reveal himself to be Luke Fox. Luke was the son of Lucius Fox, the CEO of Wayne Industries.

"Great job, Luke," Bruce said.

"Thank you," the young man replied. "I wouldn't want a full-time job as a stunt performer. But it's fun to help my friend fill out his stunt crew for a couple of days."

Bruce raised an eyebrow. "Your friend's lucky to know someone who can fight while wearing a mask."

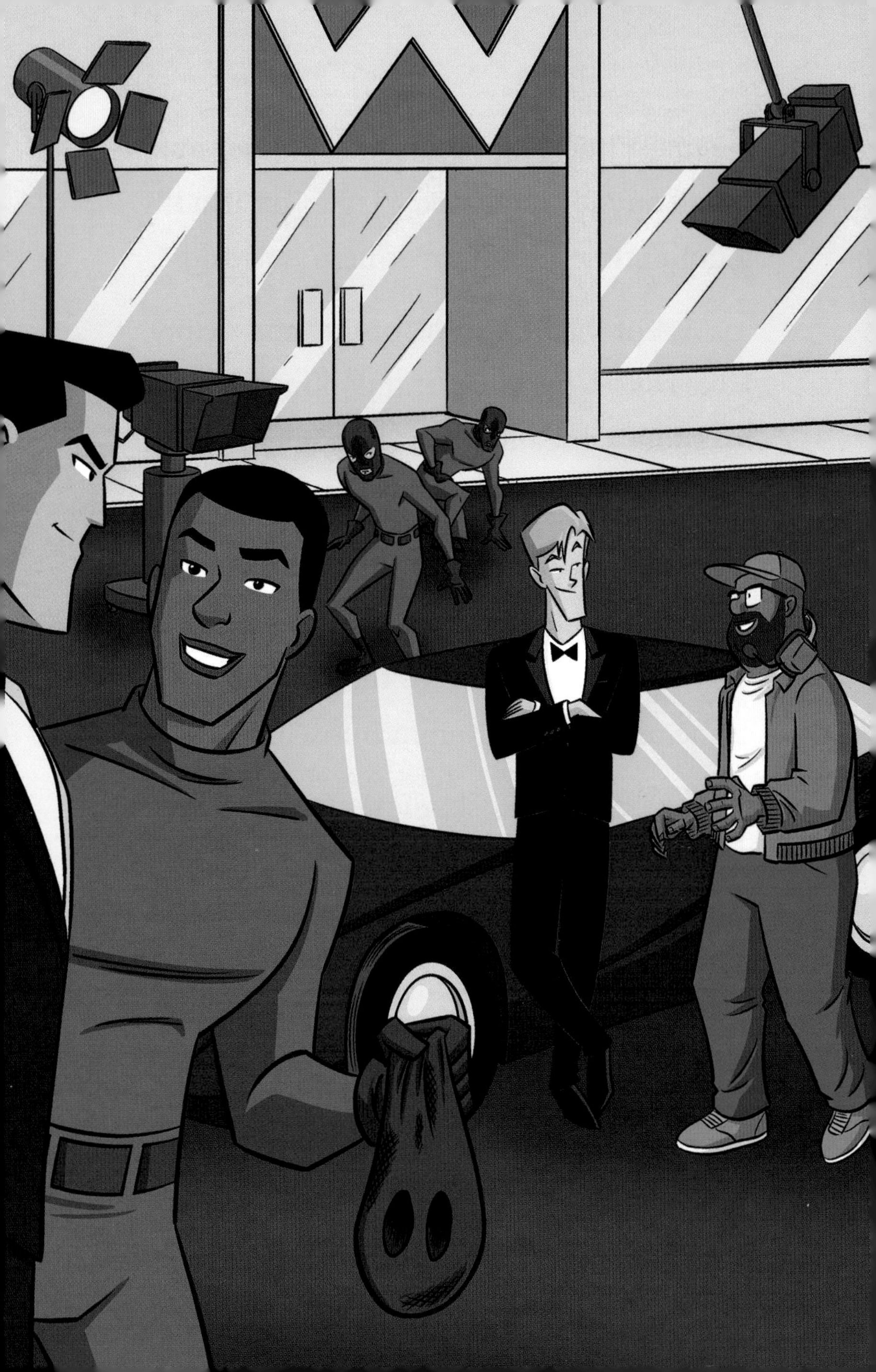

Luke chuckled. "Yeah, except I get to play a bad guy for a change." Luke Fox usually fought crime as the super hero Batwing.

"What did you think of the lead actor?" Luke asked, pointing at the man in the tuxedo. "He seemed to copy some of his moves from Batman."

Bruce nodded. "I noticed that." Of course, no one would know better, since Bruce Wayne spent most of his nights fighting crime as the Dark Knight himself.

Luke pulled his ski mask over his head. "I better get back." He joined the other four masked men by the sports car.

The director, Bill Muehl, put an arm around the tuxedoed man and led him over to Bruce. "Mr. Wayne," Bill said, "I want to thank you again for letting us use the front of Wayne Industries for this shot."

"My pleasure," Bruce said. "I enjoyed having a front row seat for all the action. It's very exciting."

"And I want to introduce you to the star of our movie," Bill continued. "Mr. Wayne, meet Mike Kagahn."

Bruce leaned forward and shook the man's hand. "Please, call me Bruce, both of you."

"Good to meet you, Bruce," said Mike. "What did you think of our little action sequence?"

"I'm impressed," Bruce replied. "And it looks like you have it covered from every angle." The billionaire pointed to the three cameras—two on the sidewalk and one perched on a window-washing platform dangling several stories up the side of the building.

The director opened his mouth to reply, but Mike cut him off. "This was a very complicated fight scene. We had to make sure that every one of my moves was perfectly recorded."

"About those moves," Bruce said. "Where did you learn . . ."

KRASH! The movie camera on the window-washing rig smashed on the sidewalk. Hundreds of feet above, the platform dangled from a single rope. One of the ropes had snapped and now two crewmembers held on for dear life.

"Oh, no!" Bill said. He raised a radio to his mouth. "Get a crane in here, fast!"

Bruce didn't know how far away the crane was, but he didn't think it would make it in time. The man and woman looked like they were losing their grips.

As Batman, he could easily fire a grapnel, swing up there, and save their lives. But as Bruce Wayne, he had to think of something else. He turned toward the sports car to somehow get Luke's attention. However, there were only four masked men standing beside the vehicle. The fifth one was missing.

WHOOOOOOSH!

A dark figure rocketed into view. It was Batwing! Blue flames blazed from his jetpack and from the bottom of his boots. He spread his arms wide, stretching out the thin wings beneath them.

Batwing angled toward the dangling crewmembers just as they lost their grip. The man and woman flailed their arms as they plummeted toward the sidewalk. The super hero swooped down and grabbed one under each arm.

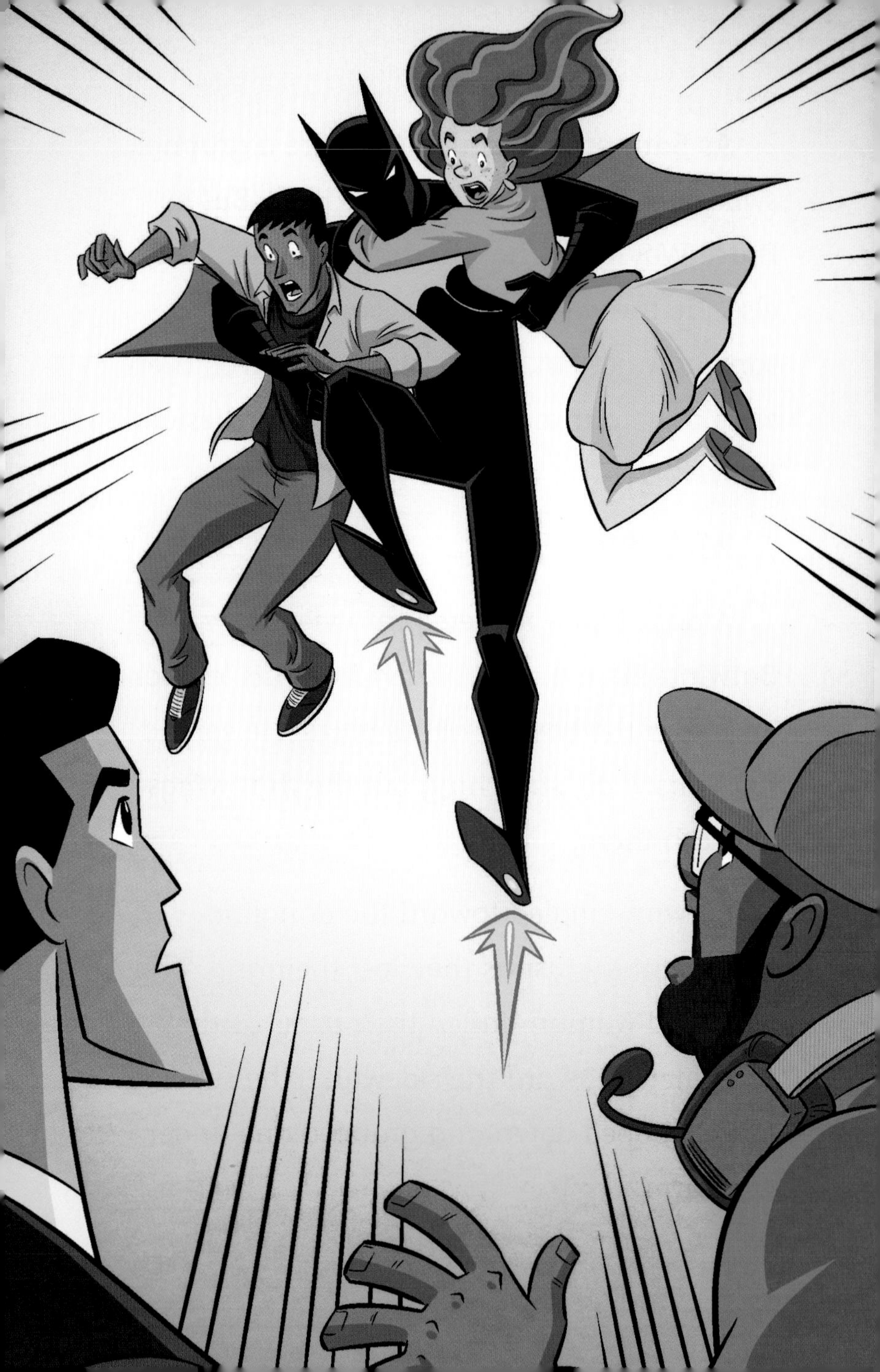

FWOOSH!

Batwing's jetpack flared as he slowed their fall. He released them after he lightly touched down on the sidewalk.

"Thank you," the woman said.

The man wiped sweat from his brow. "You really saved our bacon."

Batwing gave a nod before blasting back into the air. He zoomed away, disappearing behind the tall city buildings.

SWOOSH!

"Oh, my," Bruce said with wide eyes. "That was quite exciting. Was that part of the movie too?"

Bill shook his head. "Unfortunately, it wasn't." He turned back to the crew. "Okay, that's a wrap for today. We'll pick it up again tomorrow."

Mike Kagahn grabbed the director's arm and pulled him aside. "We can't let something like this shut us down."

"Look, I'm glad everyone's okay," Bill said. "But I'm going to have to rethink some of the scenes. This accident puts us even more behind schedule and over budget." He pointed to the broken glass and plastic bits on the sidewalk. "That camera was expensive."

"Don't worry," Mike assured him. "I'll get us more funds by tomorrow."

Bill crossed his arms. "Now, how are you going to do that?"

"I will," replied Mike. "Trust me."

CHAPTER 2

Behind-the-Scenes Bank Robbery

That night, Mike Kagahn walked down a deserted street in Gotham City. When he reached the bank, he paused and glanced around. No one was nearby, and no security cameras were in sight.

SLUUUURP! At first, the actor's face melted. Then his entire body began to change. Soon, he morphed into a huge, brown figure with bright-yellow eyes. Mike Kagahn was really Clayface!

A toothy grin stretched across the villain's face as he lowered one arm. His hand stretched and flattened until it was thin enough to slide under the bank's door. Once it was through, it stretched even farther. When it was long enough, it reached up and unlocked the door from the other side.

"All too easy," Clayface said with a chuckle. He pulled his arm out and opened the door. He stepped into the dark bank.

Clayface marched toward the giant safe in the back. He didn't bother worrying about the combination. Instead, the blob-like criminal melted until he was nothing more than a large puddle on the floor. His body slowly oozed through the thin gap beneath the thick safe door. After a few seconds, the last of him flowed out of sight.

*　*　*

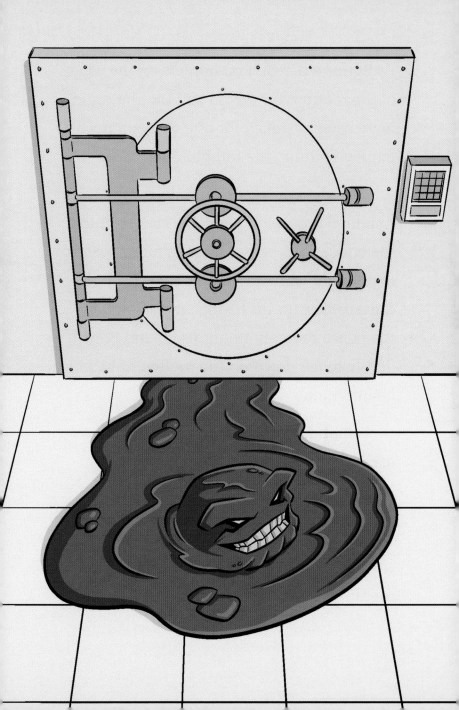

Batman perched motionless on the edge of the rooftop. He was so still that he could have been mistaken for one of the many gargoyles lining the tall building.

Even though he was unmoving, the Dark Knight was on high alert. His eyes scanned the dark streets below, looking for any signs of criminal activity. His ears monitored the tiny speakers in his headgear, listening to the police radio. Batman also heard Batwing lightly touch down on the rooftop right behind him.

"What do you have to report?" Batman asked without turning around.

"I can never sneak up on you, can I?" Batwing asked.

A smile pulled at the corners of Batman's mouth. "No. But keep trying."

Batwing strolled over to the edge of the roof. "So far, everything is quiet. Very strange for Gotham City."

Batman cocked his head, hearing an alert on the police radio. "Quiet until now," he said. "A silent alarm was tripped at a bank two blocks away." He pulled his grapnel from his Utility Belt. "The police are on the way, but we're closer."

POP!

Batman fired his grapnel into the night. When it attached to the side of another building, he leaped off the roof. Holding tightly to the thin cable, the hero swung toward the street below.

WHOOOOOSH!

Batwing's rocket pack ignited and he flew after the Dark Knight.

The super heroes landed on the sidewalk in front of the bank. Batman led the way as they marched through the open door. He pulled a flashlight from his Utility Belt and shone it around the bank. Other than the open door, everything seemed to be in order.

Batwing moved toward the large safe. "The vault's still locked," he said.

"Better check inside, just to be sure," Batman said.

Batwing knelt beside the safe and pulled out a small black box. "This is something my father has been working on." He placed the box next to the lock and numbers raced across a tiny screen. Lucius Fox invented many of Batman and Batwing's special tools, weapons, and gadgets.

KLAK!

The vault unlocked and the door began to swing open. The heroes stepped back, ready for action.

A short, older gentleman stood just inside the vault. He wore thin glasses, a three-piece suit, and an ID badge.

"Thank goodness you're here!" the man said. "My name is Trevor Plantagenet, the bank manager." The thin, gray mustache on his upper lip twitched nervously. "I feel so foolish. I accidentally locked myself inside the safe. It's all quite embarrassing."

Batman reached out and examined the badge. It confirmed what the man had said. "The police are on the way," the hero told him. "You'll have to explain everything to them."

"Oh, I will," Mr. Plantagenet agreed. "You can be certain of that."

The super heroes left the bank and waited on a nearby rooftop. They watched as two patrol cars arrived. Their blue and red lights flashed over the building as four police officers got out and questioned the man from the vault.

"Accidentally trapped in the vault," Batwing said. "Didn't that seem a little suspicious?"

"It did," agreed Batman. "But I ran his name through the Batcomputer on our way to the roof." The Dark Knight held up a small device showing the man's image on a tiny screen. "Trevor Plantagenet really is the manager of this bank."

Batwing shrugged. "Then we're still hanging around because . . ."

"I'm not sure," Batman replied. "Call it a hunch."

Batwing pointed to a figure running down the sidewalk toward the bank. "Could that be your hunch arriving now?"

Batman's eyes locked in on the figure. It was Trevor Plantagenet, except now he was dressed in pajamas, slippers, and a bathrobe.

Batman's eyes narrowed. "I have a feeling *that* is the real bank manager."

"Then who was trapped in the vault?" Batwing asked.

Batman stepped to the edge of the roof and leaped off. "Let's find out." He spread his cape wide, gliding toward the sidewalk. Batwing was close behind.

The heroes touched down just as the man in the bathrobe ran up to the police officers.

"What's going on here?" the man asked, nearly out of breath.

The officers glanced at the new arrival and then at the man from the vault. They were seeing double.

The Trevor Plantagenet wearing the suit grinned. "What can I say? You got me." His eyes flashed yellow just before he exploded into Clayface. The giant blob of a criminal towered over the crowd.

The police officers flew backward, but Batman and Batwing charged forward.

WHOOSH!

Batwing took to the air, getting the villain's attention. Clayface shot long, muddy tendrils at the flying super hero but missed every time.

Meanwhile, Batman punched the squishy criminal's stomach. **SPOOSH!** His arm sank up to his elbow.

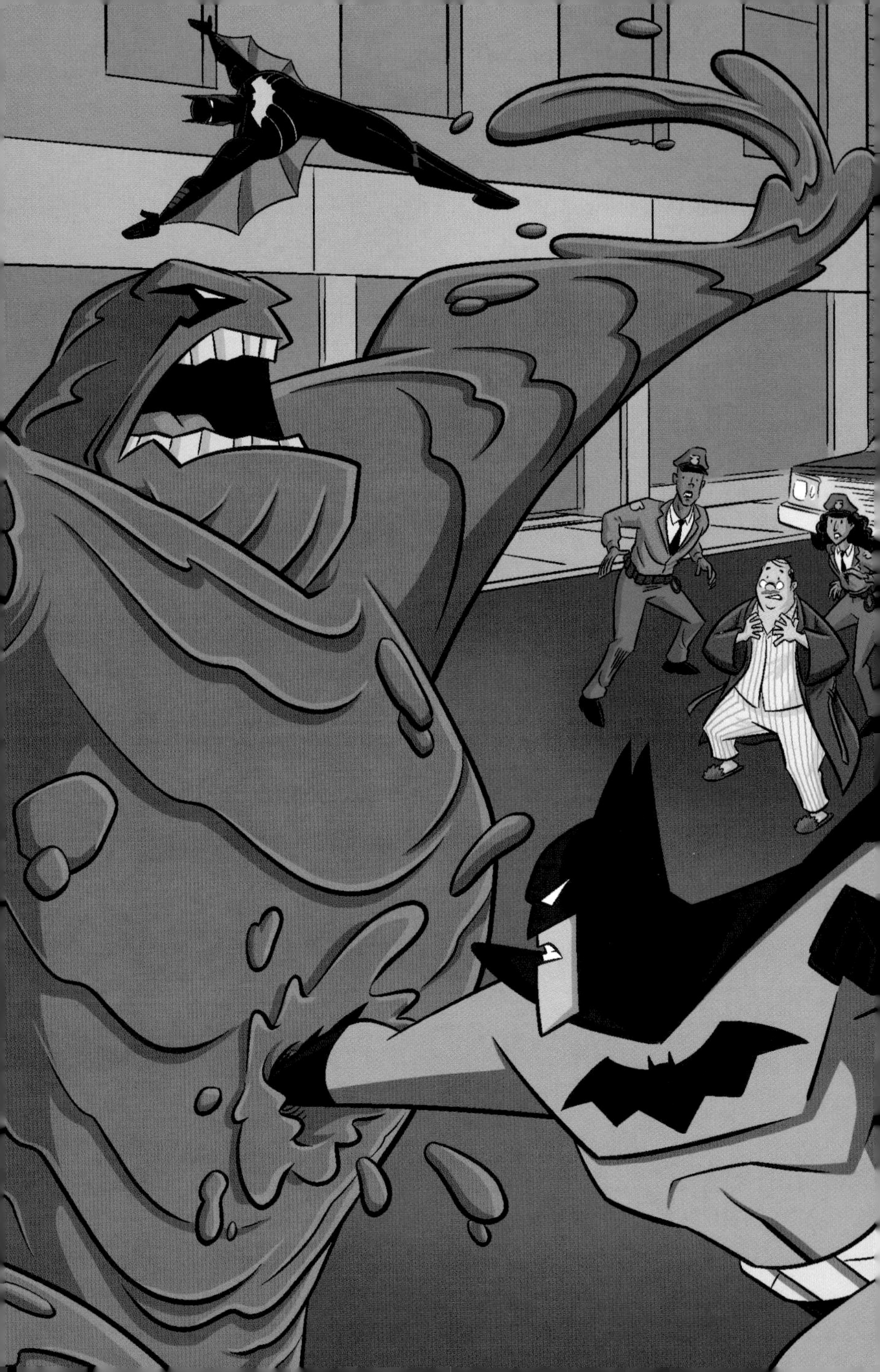

But the Dark Knight wasn't trying to hurt Clayface. He was looking for something. With a loud **SLURP**, Batman removed his arm and pulled out a large bag of cash stolen from the bank vault.

"Not so fast, Bats," Clayface said. "I stole it first."

The criminal formed his right hand into a giant mallet and swung at the Dark Knight. Batman flipped back, barely dodging the blow. Unfortunately, he didn't see the thin tendril snaking up and around the bag of cash. It jerked the bag free from the crime fighter's grasp.

PTEW! Batwing swooped in and fired a Batarang from his wrist. It sliced through the tendril before Clayface could pull it back in.

Clayface roared with anger and shot something back at the flying hero.

SPLAT!

A glob of clay covered the hero's mask. He couldn't see, and he couldn't pull it away from his face.

"Now there's an idea," Clayface said as he sent blobs flying at the police officers.

SPLAT! SPLAT-SPLAT! SPLAT!

Brown globs covered the officers' mouths and noses. They could all see, but they couldn't breathe! Their eyes widened as they struggled to pull the sticky substance from their faces.

"Hold on!" Batman ordered. He reached for his Utility Belt as he ran toward the struggling officers. He pulled out a small canister and sprayed the brown glob on one of the victims.

FZZZZZZ!

The white spray—based on freeze tech from the villain Mr. Freeze—hardened the clay instantly. The barrier cracked and crumbled away. The officer gasped for air as Batman moved to help the next victim.

As Batman freed the last officer, Batwing raised a hand to his own covered face. The same white spray blasted from a nozzle on his wrist, freezing his glob of clay.

Unfortunately, by the time everyone was free, Clayface and the stolen money were nowhere to be found.

CHAPTER 3

Performer Plot Twist

KLIK·KLAK·KLAK·KLIK!

The next day, Batman's fingers flew over the keyboard as he researched data on the Batcomputer. One by one, photographs of ten banks popped onto the screen. They floated over a map of Gotham City. Each bank matched the description that Batman had entered into the computer. Each bank had been robbed in the same way—late at night, after the bank was closed for the day.

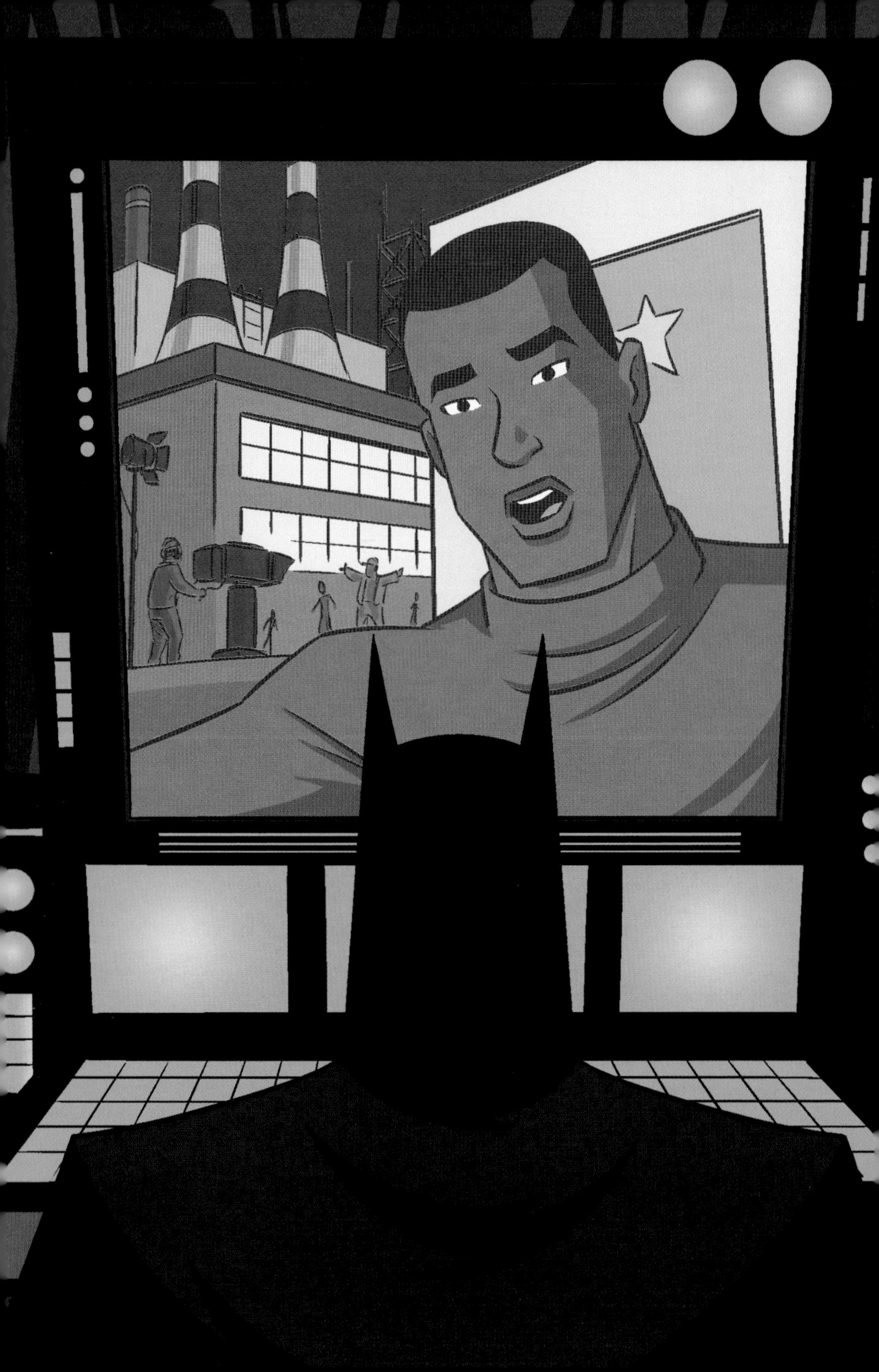

The Dark Knight flicked a switch and an image of Luke Fox appeared on the screen. He was on the movie set for another day of shooting. This time they were filming at an old oil refinery. Several crewmembers set up equipment behind him.

"Can you talk?" Batman asked.

Luke glanced over his right shoulder, before ducking behind a stack of large pipes. "I can now."

"I found a series of bank robberies similar to the one from last night," Batman explained. "When did the movie begin production?"

"Two weeks ago," Luke replied. "Why?"

"Because that's when the robberies stopped," the Dark Knight replied. "That is, until Clayface hit the bank last night."

"Do you think he's involved with the movie somehow?" Luke asked.

"Clayface used to be an actor named Matt Hagen," Batman explained. "This could be his way of making a comeback."

"But why rob the bank last night?" Luke asked.

"I heard the director complain about how much that accident had cost them," Batman replied.

"Matt Hagen, Mike Kagahn," Luke said. "I bet he is trying to make a comeback. I'll snoop around the set and see what I can find out."

The Dark Knight nodded. "Good idea. But don't make a move until I get there. I'm on my way."

* * *

Luke switched off his phone and shoved it into his pocket. He moved through the set looking for anything suspicious.

The old oil refinery was alive with activity as everyone set up lights and cameras. A fire truck and a helicopter waited nearby. The helicopter was going to be part of the scene. But the firefighters were there for safety, since some special effects explosions would be used in the upcoming action.

Luke moved through the crew until he spotted Bill Muehl. The director entered one of the trailers near the back of the refinery.

Luke jogged toward the trailer and spotted a star on the door with Mike Kagahn's name printed beneath it.

"I wonder if the director is in on it too," Luke said as he slid on a black glove. It was from his Batwing uniform.

Luke tried to act casual as he leaned against the trailer, gently placing two fingers on the window. The fingertips held tiny microchips that picked up sound vibrations on the glass—another gadget developed by his dad.

"I don't know how you did it, Mike, my boy," Bill's voice said in Luke's earpiece. "But this money makes up for the broken camera and then some."

"There's plenty more where that came from," Mike replied. "I want this movie to be a success more than anyone."

"I would say so," Bill said. "Since you're paying for everything."

Luke heard footsteps inside the trailer, so he quickly backed off. He was several feet away when the door opened. Bill and Mike stepped out.

So, Mike Kagahn is funding the entire movie, Luke thought. *That's unusual for an actor, but not for a bank-robbing super-villain.*

Luke followed the two as they walked toward the rest of the crew.

Even though Batman said to wait, Luke thought, *there has to be a way to find out if Kagahn is Clayface or not.*

Luke grabbed a bottle of water from a table that held snacks for the crew. He unscrewed the cap before moving closer to the actor.

This will probably get me fired from the movie, Luke thought. *But here goes . . .*

When he was close to Mike, Luke squeezed his water bottle. *SPLOOSH!* Water gushed from the bottle and splashed all over the actor's face.

"Ahhh!" the actor shouted in surprise. "I can't believe this!"

"Oh no! Sorry about that, Mr. Kagahn," Luke said.

Bill jumped back in shock. "What's wrong with your face, Mike?"

Mike put a hand to his face—his melting face. His eyes flashed yellow and he growled with anger.

"You bumbling fool!" the actor shouted. "Now you've ruined everything!"

EEK! AHH! Several crewmembers screamed as Mike Kagahn instantly morphed into Clayface.

Luke leaped over the snack table as the villain raised his giant fists to pound him.

KRASH!

The clay criminal smashed the table instead, sending peanuts, water bottles, and candy flying everywhere. The rest of the movie crew ran for their lives.

That proved my theory, Luke thought as he, too, ran for cover. *Now I just need to keep from being pounded long enough to change into Batwing.*

VROOOOOM!

The Batmobile roared to a stop as the hatch slid open. The Dark Knight flew out of the vehicle, a handful of Batarangs at the ready.

WHIP·WHIP·WHIP·WHIP!

The bat-shaped weapons flew through the air and stuck all over the clay villain. They didn't stop Clayface. But they distracted him long enough for Luke to get away.

"Why can't you just leave me alone?" Clayface asked as he charged toward the hero. "All I want is my own action movie. It's bad enough I can't even use my real name anymore."

Clayface formed both fists into giant, spiked balls and swung at the Dark Knight.

"That would be fine, Hagan," Batman said as he dodged the attacks, "if you didn't have to rob banks to pay for it."

Clayface raised both spikes high above his head. "What can I say? Movies aren't exactly cheap these days."

WHOOOOOSH!

"Well this movie is wrapped," Batwing said as he flew into view. He hovered behind Clayface and aimed one arm at him.

PTOW!

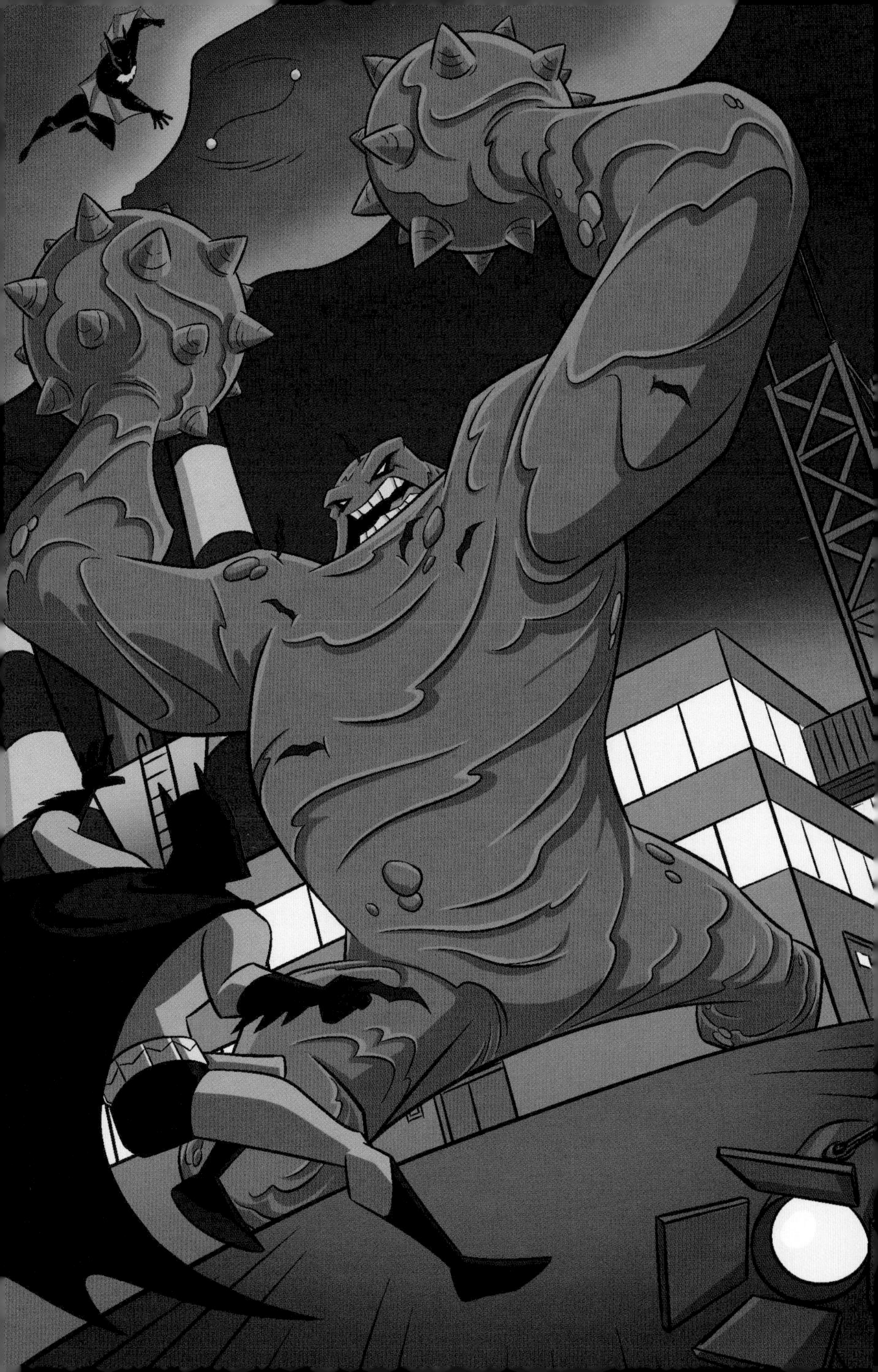

A pair of bolas shot from Batwing's wrist. The two balls connected by a thin rope encircled the villain's arms, stopping him from smashing Batman.

Clayface laughed as his wrists shrank and the bolas fell harmlessly to the ground. Then, with lightning speed, he shot an arm up at Batwing.

SLOOSH!

The thin tendril quickly snaked around the flying hero, wrapping him tightly. Clayface performed the same move on Batman before the Dark Knight could get clear. The villain laughed as he dragged both crime fighters closer.

"I always wondered what it would be like to have a little hero in me," Clayface said.

SLUUUUUURP!

The villain pulled Batman and Batwing completely into his body. They tried to break free, but they couldn't punch or kick their way out of his muddy chest.

"Listen up, everyone!" Clayface shouted at the cowering crew. "As soon as these two bats run out of air, we finish this movie." A toothy grin stretched across his face. "Anyone who doesn't like it gets the same treatment."

CHAPTER 4

Real-Time Remake

"Go, go, go!" Bill told the pilot as he scrambled aboard the helicopter. The pilot quickly flicked switches and the main rotor began to spin.

WHOOSH! WHOOSH! WHOOSH!

Clayface spotted the helicopter as it began to leave the ground. "Where do you think you're going, Bill?" the villain shouted. "I'm ready for my close-up!"

Clayface extended a long tendril toward the aircraft. The snakelike arm wrapped around one of the helicopter's skids. It slammed the craft back to the ground.

While the clay criminal was distracted, the firefighters unrolled a long hose and started the fire truck's pump. A firefighter chuckled as she aimed the nozzle at Clayface's back.

"We get to save Batman and Batwing for a change," she said as she cranked the valve open and . . .

BOOOOOOSHH!

A stream of water blasted the giant criminal. Clayface roared with frustration as the water turned much of his body into mud. Two clay-covered crime fighters fell out of his torso and rolled across the ground. The firefighters cheered as Batman and Batwing stumbled to their feet.

"Thanks," Batman told the firefighters.

The helicopter took to the air once more. This time, Clayface didn't try to stop it. Instead, the half-melted criminal tromped toward it. He stretched out his arm and latched onto the skid once more. Then he pulled himself off the ground and snaked into the helicopter. Within moments, Bill and the pilot were thrown from the craft. They screamed as they plummeted toward the ground.

"I'm on it," Batwing said as his jetpack fired. He spread his arms wide and flew toward the falling people. He swooped them up with ease and headed back toward the ground.

Meanwhile, Batman pulled out his grapnel and fired at the helicopter.

POP-KLANK!

The claw latched onto the helicopter just before it flew out of range. The Dark Knight was jerked from his feet as the craft soared higher and higher.

Batman hit the thumb switch and his grapnel retracted. The thin cable wound tightly, pulling the hero toward the chopper at amazing speed.

As he reached the craft, Batman swung out his legs and released the grapnel. He flew into the cockpit, kicking Clayface out of the pilot's seat. The villain latched onto the side of the helicopter before falling to the ground.

"You ruined everything!" Clayface roared as he turned an arm into a long spike. He jabbed it at the Dark Knight.

Batman barely dodged the stabbing point as he held on to the helicopter. The spinning craft flew out of control over Gotham City.

The Dark Knight wedged a Batarang against the base of the control stick. As the craft pulled up, he touched the side of his head to activate a communicator.

"Batwing, get to the helicopter," Batman said. "Make sure it doesn't crash."

Without waiting for a reply, Batman leapt at Clayface. He slammed into the criminal and they tumbled from the helicopter. Batman reached for his grapnel, but Clayface stopped him. The criminal's body liquefied and wrapped around the Dark Knight.

"I do all my own stunts," Clayface said with a laugh. "Let's see how you do with a fall from this height."

Completely covered in clay, Batman tumbled to the city below.

KRASH!

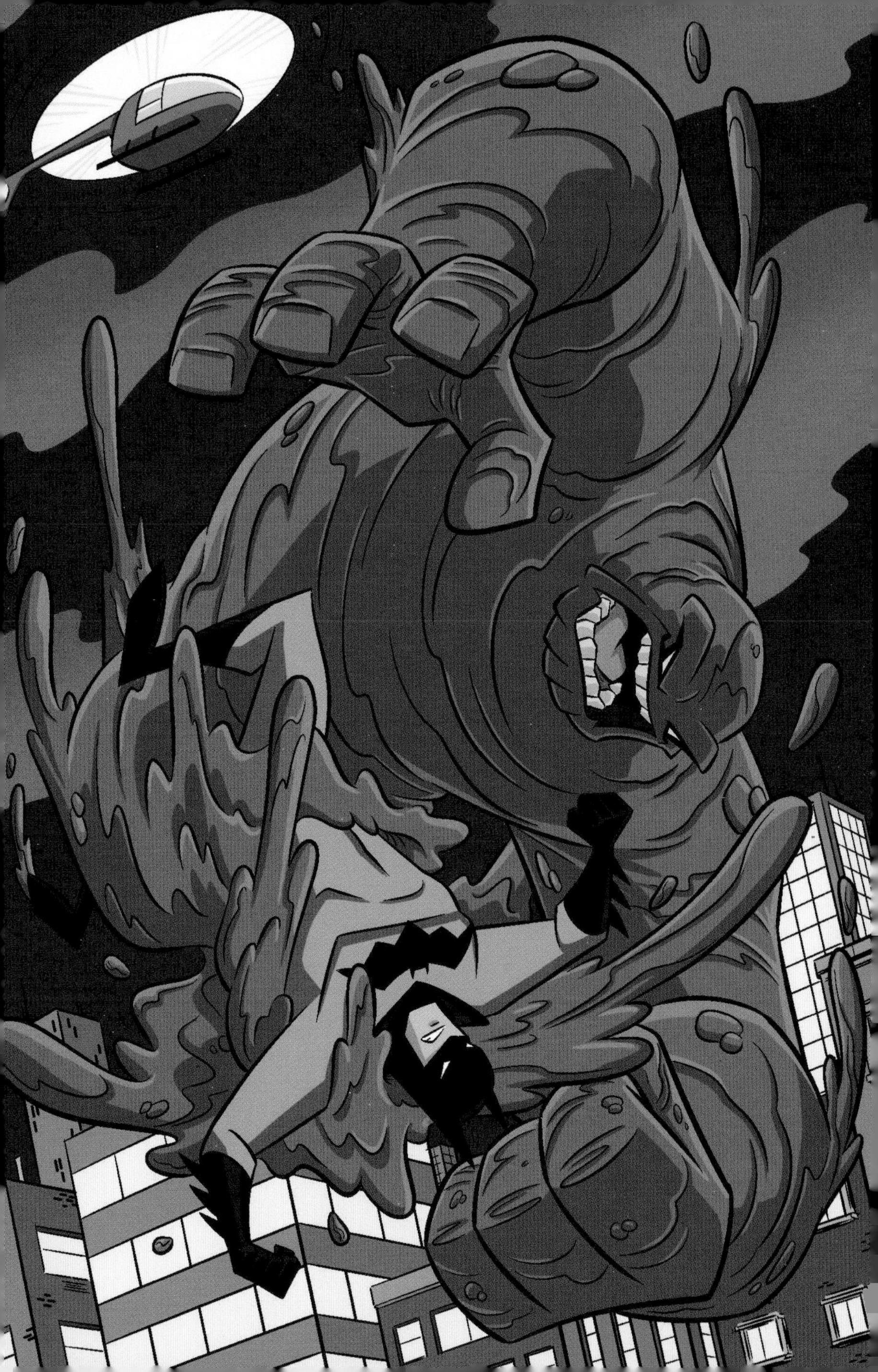

They smashed through a skylight and landed in a dark room. Clayface slithered away before Batman could get to his feet.

Dazed, the Dark Knight was startled by a man with a sharp sword, poised to strike. Batman prepared to fend off the attack when he noticed two things. One: the man was actually Genghis Khan, an ancient Mongolian warlord. And two: he was nothing more than a wax figure.

As Batman's eyes adjusted to the light, he realized that they had landed in Professor Hornswallow's world-famous wax museum. He was surrounded by dozens of historical wax figures.

"All I wanted was my acting career back," Clayface's voice echoed throughout the museum. "I was the best, I tell ya! I could play anybody!"

Suddenly, one of the figures sprang to life. Batman barely had time to duck as an armored man swung a long sword at his head. It was Clayface as a medieval knight.

KLING! KLANG!

Batman blocked two more blows with his spiked gauntlets. Then the armored knight disappeared back into the darkness.

"I was so good, you would never know it was me," Clayface added.

SWOOOSH!

Batman flipped backward as a Japanese samurai sliced the air in front of him. The hero dodged three sword swipes before kicking the samurai back into the shadows.

"I studied the moves and fighting styles of so many characters," Clayface's voice continued.

WHOOOSH!

Batman barely dodged the tip of a sharp spear as a centurion attacked.

WHIP-WHIP-WHIP!

Batman flung three Batarangs. The soldier blocked two, but the third knocked the spear from his hand. Then the Roman fighter charged Batman with his shield. The Dark Knight caught the weapon and flipped the centurion back into the dark museum.

Clayface returned as a Zulu warrior . . .

SHING! KLANG!

. . . and then as a Viking.

SWOOOSH! KLING! KLANG!

Each time, Batman fended off attacks before the villain disappeared into the shadows.

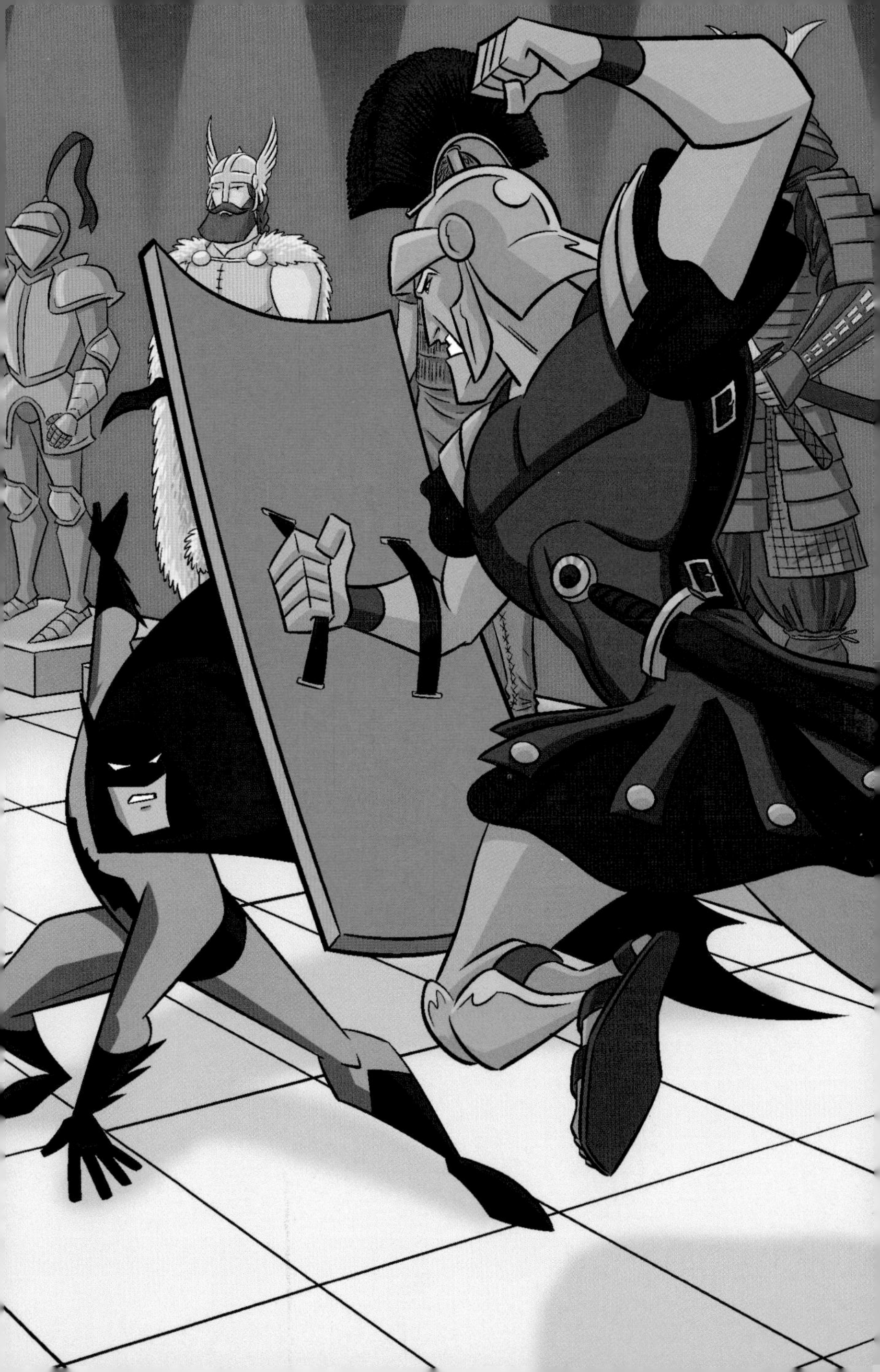

"I've even studied your fighting style," Clayface's voice continued. "Say, that's an idea. Perhaps, I can play someone a little more . . . up-to-date."

The Caped Crusader readied himself as the next warrior came in for an attack. When Clayface's new character stepped into the light, Batman couldn't believe his eyes.

CHAPTER 5

Stunt Double Trouble

Batwing reached the helicopter and plopped into the pilot's seat. He grabbed the stick and grunted as he struggled with the controls. The aircraft finally stopped spinning and leveled out. Batwing let out a sigh of relief as he landed the helicopter on an empty rooftop.

The super hero flew out of the helicopter and hovered over the city. He scanned the area, looking for where Batman and Clayface went down.

Moments later, Batwing spotted the broken skylight and headed for it. As he flew closer, he recognized the outside of the Gotham City Wax Museum. He had visited it many times, but had never entered through the skylight before.

Once inside, Batwing spotted one of the strangest things he'd ever seen. He saw Batman fighting it out with . . . Batman!

The two Caped Crusaders seemed evenly matched as they traded blows. They countered each other's kicks, punches, and flips. Batwing touched down a few feet away from the battling super heroes.

"Good, you're here," one Batman said. "Help me defeat Clayface."

"Don't listen to him," the other Batman ordered. "*He's* Clayface."

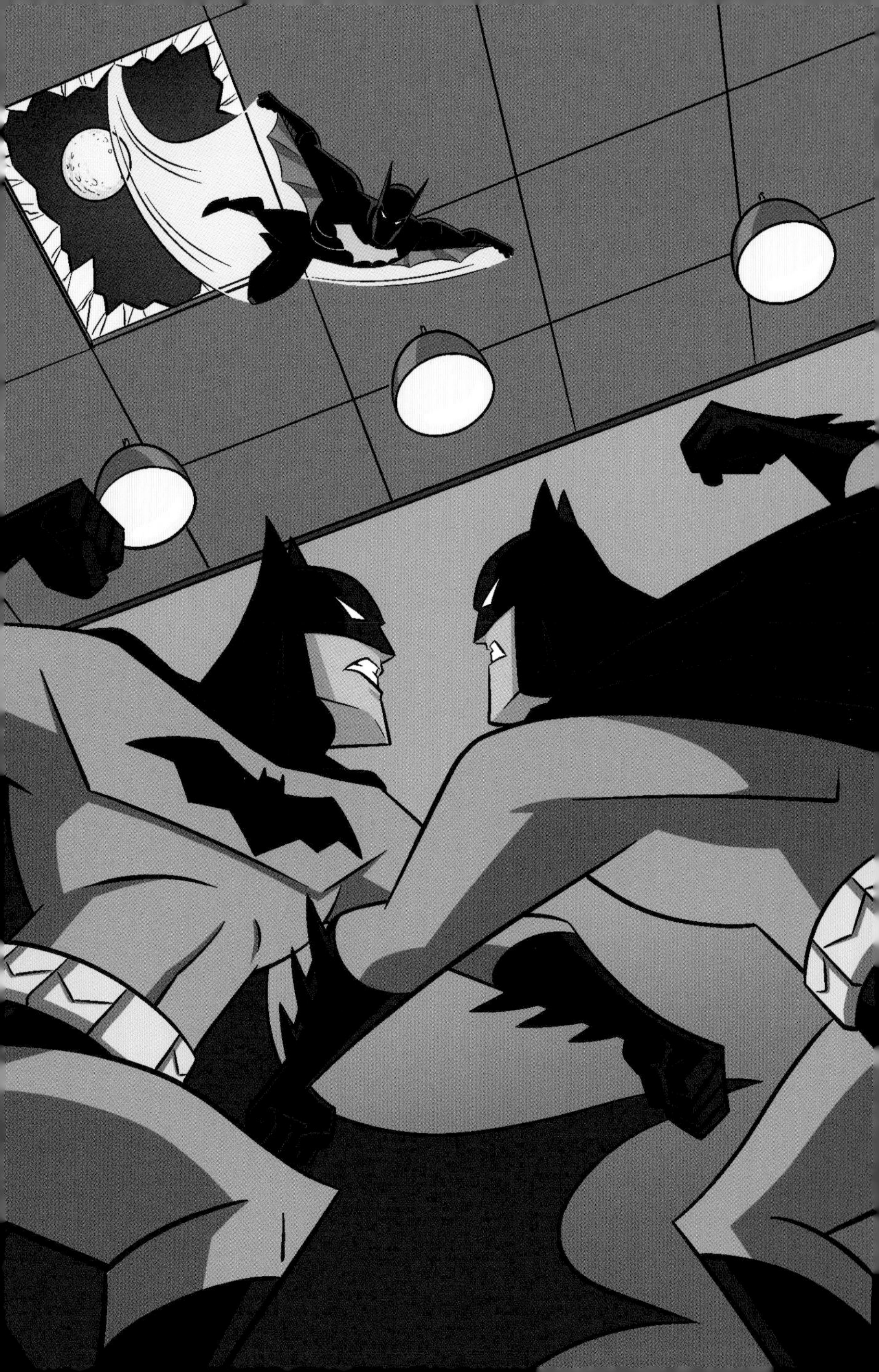

Batwing shook his head. "I can't tell you apart."

"He's obviously studied my fighting style," said the Batman on the left. He performed a spinning kick.

"Making us even harder to tell apart," finished the Batman on the right. He easily blocked the kick before performing one of his own.

"All right," Batwing said, crossing his arms. "How did you and I defeat Bane at Gotham City Stadium that time?"

"Good thinking, Batwing," said one Batman.

"Except several baseball fans recorded our fight with their phones," the other Batman pointed out. "Clayface could have seen one of those videos online."

One Batman launched himself toward the other. He slammed into the other Batman's torso and they tumbled across the floor. Several wax figures fell like bowling pins before the twin crime fighters sprang to their feet once more.

There has to be some way to tell them apart, Batwing thought. *Or at least a way to defeat Clayface that won't harm Batman.*

Batwing quickly raised an arm and fired a Batarang from his wrist.

WHIP!

The sharp weapon zipped across the room and sliced off a corner of one battling Batman's cape. A tiny, black piece of cloth floated to the ground.

Ah-ha! Batwing thought. *Now I know who is who.*

If the Batman with the sliced cape had been Clayface, the severed cloth would have turned back into clay. But since it didn't change, that meant that Batwing had cut the real Batman's cape.

The two versions of Batman continued to fight and Batwing prepared to help his fellow crime fighter. Unfortunately, as Batwing prepared to fire another Batarang, something stopped him in his tracks.

Now both Dark Knights had a corner missing from their capes. Clayface had copied the flaw, and both Caped Crusaders were identical once more.

Batwing scanned the area for anything that might be helpful. He knew the museum well, so there had to be something. That's when he remembered one of his favorite exhibits.

"Too bad the World's Greatest Detective can't meet the world's greatest escape artist," Batwing said.

"Good idea," said one Batman. He flipped away from the other Batman's kick. Then he turned and ran into another part of the wax museum.

"Hurry, Batwing," said the second Batman as he chased after the first. "We can't let Clayface get away!"

The young hero followed, but he knew exactly who the real Batman was now.

When he entered the next room, Batwing spotted Batman—the real Batman—standing atop a tall glass box. The second Batman leaped into the air, somersaulted, and landed atop the box next to the first.

THUNK!

Batwing raised an arm and fired a pair of bolas at the second Batman. They wrapped around him just after he landed.

"What are you doing, Batwing?" the second Batman asked. His arms were pinned to his sides. "Can't you tell? I'm the real Batman."

Batwing shook his head. "Nice try. But I don't think so."

"Otherwise you would've known about the world's greatest escape artist," Batman added as he hopped off the glass box.

HA! HA! HA! HA! The bound Batman laughed and his eyes flashed bright yellow.

"World's greatest escape artist?" Clayface mused. As he morphed back into his villainous form, the bolas dropped to the ground. "Oh, yeah. That must be me."

"Guess again," Batman said as he pulled a lever on the side of the box.

The platform beneath the criminal's feet dropped away. Clayface fell into the glass box, which was actually a glass tank—full of water.

SPLOOSH!

The tank was a copy of the one belonging to Harry Houdini—the magician and world's greatest escape artist. Houdini would often escape the tank full of water while wearing a straitjacket. In fact, a wax figure of the magician, straitjacket and all, stood in front of the tank.

"No!" Clayface shouted as he splashed inside the tank, trying to escape. You can't do this to me!"

KA-THUNK!

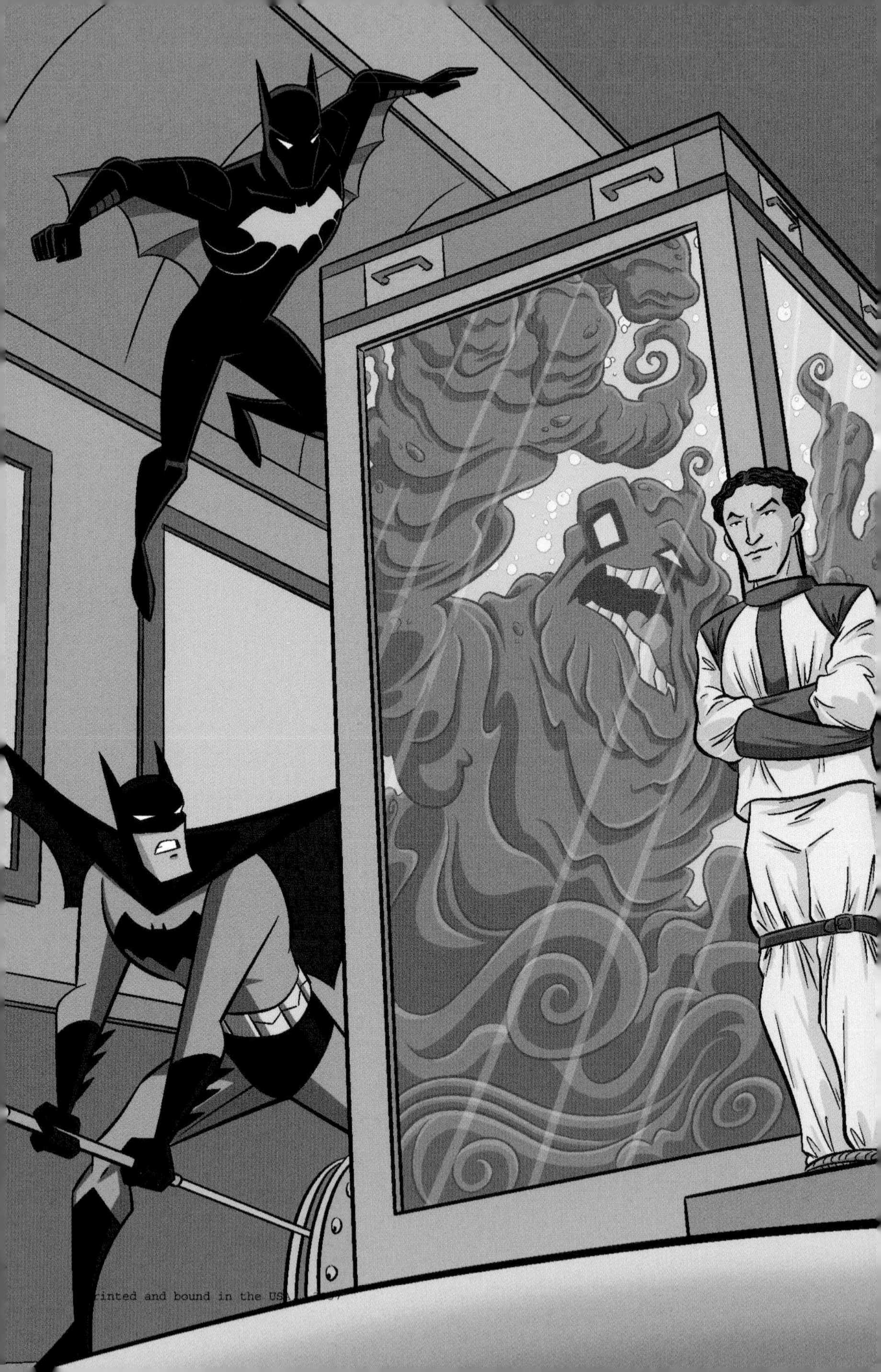

rinted and bound in the USA

Batman pushed the lever back, sealing the hatch above Clayface. As the water churned, it slowly dissolved the villain. In seconds, the tank held nothing more than a brown, muddy mess.

"Clayface is no Houdini," Batwing said. "So that tank should hold him a while."

"All the way to Blackgate Prison," Batman added.

Printed and bound in the USA.   3837

Clayface

REAL NAME: Matt Hagen

OCCUPATION: Professional Criminal

BASE: Gotham City

HEIGHT: Varies

WEIGHT: Varies

EYES: Varies

HAIR: Varies

POWERS/ABILITIES:
Shape-shifting and
superhuman strength.
He is also a professional
actor and skilled
impressionist.

BIOGRAPHY:

Formerly a big name in the movie industry, actor Matt Hagen had his face, and career, ruined in a tragic car crash. Hoping to regain his good looks, Hagan accepted the help of ruthless businessman Roland Daggett, who gave him a special cream that allowed Hagen to reshape his face like clay. Hopelessly addicted, Hagen was caught stealing more cream, and Daggett forced him to consume an entire barrel as punishment. However, instead of killing Hagen, the large dose turned him into a monster with only one thing on his muddy mind: revenge.

- As Clayface, Matt Hagen is no longer human. His entire body is made of clay, which grants him shape-shifting abilities as well as super-strength.

- Clayface's power is limited only by his imagination. He can turn his limbs into lethal weapons by willing his muddy body into whatever shape he desires.

- Drawing upon his shape-shifting abilities and his experience as an actor, Clayface assumes the shapes and voices of others. These abilities make him a very difficult foe to detect.

BIOGRAPHIES

Author

Michael Anthony Steele has been writing for television, movies, and video games for more than 27 years. He has authored more than 120 books for exciting characters and brands including Batman, Superman, Wonder Woman, Scooby-Doo, LEGO City, Garfield, *Winx Club*, *Night at the Museum*, and *The Penguins of Madagascar*. Mr. Steele lives on a ranch in Texas, but he enjoys meeting his readers when he visits schools and libraries all across the country. For more information, visit MichaelAnthonySteele.com

Illustrator

Gregg Schigiel is the creator/author/illustrator of the superhero/fairy tale mash-up Pix graphic novels and was a regular contributor to Spongebob Comics. Outside of work, Mr. Schigiel bakes prize-winning cookies, enjoys comedy, and makes sure he drinks plenty of water. Learn more at greggschigiel.com.

GLOSSARY

bola (BOW-la)—a throwing weapon made of weighted balls connected by cords

CEO (SEE-EEE-OH)—short for "chief executive officer"; a CEO is the leader of a company

combination (kahm-buh-NAY-shun)—a sequence of numbers or letters used to open a lock

gargoyle (GAR-goil)—a make-believe creature made of stone

grapnel (GRAP-nuhl)—a grappling hook connected to a rope that can be fired like a gun

microchip (MYE-kroh-chip)—a tiny circuit that processes information in a computer

morph (MORF)—to change from one form to another

refinery (ri-FINE-uhr-ee)—a place where petroleum is made into gasoline, motor oil, and other products

straitjacket (STRAYT-jak-it)—a garment made of strong material designed to bind the arms of a violent or disoriented person

tendril (TEN-drel)—a long, thin, curling stem that helps plants attach to and climb up buildings

tuxedo (tuhk-SEE-doh)—a man's jacket, usually black with satin lapels, worn with a bow tie for formal occasions

DISCUSSION QUESTIONS

1. Batman teams up with Batwing in this story. What makes Batwing different from some of Batman's other sidekicks, such as Robin, Batgirl, or Batwoman?

2. When Batman and Batwing get trapped inside Clayface, the firefighters come to their rescue. Do you think the heroes would have been able to escape without their help? Explain your answer.

3. In the wax museum, Clayface changes into many different historical warriors. If you could change into a warrior from the past, which one would you choose, and why?

WRITING PROMPTS

1. Clayface can change the shape of his body in any way he likes. If you had this ability, how would you use it for good? Write a paragraph describing how you would help people with your power.

2. Batwing uses a variety of gadgets created by his father, Lucius Fox. If you could invent a cool crime-fighting tool, what would it be? Write a short description explaining how your gadget works and draw a picture of it.

3. At the end of the story, Batman says Clayface will be taken to Blackgate Prison. But what if he escapes on the way there? Write a new chapter describing how Clayface escapes and what the villain does next.

LOOK FOR MORE
DC SUPER HERO ADVENTURES